MW00998299

What Animal Needs a Wig?

Funny Riddles and Interesting Facts

By
Abigail Fuller
and Neil Wollman

Illustrated by
Frances Baldwin

STAR BRIGHT BOOKS

Cambridge, Massachusetts

"For Leo, Jack, Beau, and–especially and always–Scout." –Abigail and Neil

"To Mom and Dad, who generously shared with their children a love for books." –Fran B.

Text copyright © 2014 Abigail A. Fuller and Neil Wollman
Illustrations copyright © 2014 Frances Fuller Baldwin

All rights reserved. No part of this book may be reproduced or transmitted in any form or by any means, electronic or mechanical, photocopying, recording, or by any information storage and retrieval systems that are available now or in the future, without permission in writing from the copyright holders and the publisher.

Published in the United States of America by Star Bright Books, Inc.
The name Star Bright Books and the Star Bright Books logo are registered trademarks of Star Bright Books, Inc. Please visit: www.starbrightbooks.com.
For bulk orders, email: orders@starbrightbooks.com, or call customer service at: (617) 354-1300.

Paperback ISBN-13: 978-1-59572-677-3
Star Bright Books / MA / 00110140
Printed in the U.S.A. (Kase Printing) 10 9 8 7 6 5 4 3 2 1

Printed on paper from sustainable forests and a percentage of post-consumer paper.

Library of Congress Cataloging-in-Publication Data

Fuller, Abigail A.
 What animal needs a wig? : funny riddles and interesting facts / by Abigail A. Fuller and Neil Wollman ; illustrated by Frances Fuller Baldwin.
    pages cm
 ISBN 978-1-59572-677-3 (pbk. : alk. paper)
 1. Animals--Juvenile literature. I. Wollman, Neil. II. Baldwin, Frances Fuller, illustrator. III. Title.
QL49.F939 2014
590.2'07--dc23
                        2014026265

What animal does a baby like to play with?

A rattlesnake

A rattlesnake makes a rattling sound when it is threatened. This is its way of warning other animals (including us!) to stay away. How do they do it? At the end of a rattlesnake's tail are small segments made of keratin, just like fingernails. When a rattlesnake vibrates its tail, the segments hit against each other and make a rattling sound. Each time a rattlesnake sheds its skin, the end bit of the old skin remains attached at the tail and becomes a new "rattle." The older rattlesnakes tend to have more rattles. Newborn rattlesnakes have a button where their first rattle will develop.

A close-up of the rattles on a tail of a rattlesnake

Rattlesnakes are so successful at scaring off other animals that some other snakes imitate them. The king snake and the milk snake both make a rattling sound by shaking their tails against dry leaves. The bull snake (or gopher snake) breathes in and out quickly to "rattle" and at the same time shakes its tail like a rattlesnake.

Rattlesnakes are found throughout America, but they are most numerous in the southwestern United States and Mexico. The bite of a rattlesnake is venomous, but it will only bite to defend itself. The best way to stay safe in rattlesnake country is to avoid surprising it: be careful turning over rocks and logs, walk instead of run, and keep your dog on a leash.

What animal is the most religious?

A praying mantis

The praying mantis gets its name because of its large front legs. The legs are bent and held up together, and it looks like the insect is praying. It would be more accurate to call it a "preying" mantis because what it actually does with its front legs—which have spikes on them—is stab and then grasp its prey. A praying mantis can kill a hummingbird by spearing it.

Praying mantises are found in warm regions all around the world, and there are over 2,000 different species. In the United States, 20 different species of praying mantis are found.

Praying mantises have enormous appetites. If there is no food available when they hatch, they will eat each other. Even adults will eat one another!

Praying mantises are a happy sight for farmers because they eat insects like aphids, grasshoppers, and beetles that destroy crops. The praying mantis is one type of bio-control insect ("good" insects that farmers use to get rid of "bad" insects). This way farmers do not have to use chemicals, which can harm wildlife like bees, frogs, and birds. The praying mantis also eats moths and crickets, and it is the only insect quick enough to catch mosquitoes and flies.

What animal is the most valuable?

A goldfish

Since goldfish are not really made of gold, they are not very valuable. You can buy one for about a dollar. The equipment necessary to care for them (a fish tank, water filter, food) is expensive. Goldfish are the most popular fish in homes and in aquariums. They were first kept as pets over 1,000 years ago in China, where they were kept in ponds. They were first brought to the United States in the 1800s and became popular pets.

Koi are related to goldfish. Both are types of carp. Koi are much larger than goldfish, and they can grow up to 3 feet in length. Koi are very colorful and often mottled with red, yellow, white, and black markings. They are usually kept in ponds outside. Unlike goldfish, koi can be very expensive. The highest price paid for a koi fish was over $2 million!

In many places it is illegal to release goldfish—or any fish—into the wild. This is because they can reproduce rapidly and threaten native fish by eating their food supplies. Because goldfish feed on the bottom of ponds, they stir up dirt in the water, blocking out the sun so the plants in the water die.

The most expensive animal ever sold was a racehorse named Green Monkey, which cost $16 million. You can buy a white lion cub if you have $138,000, but in most places it is illegal to have one because they grow big and dangerous. You can get dogs and cats for free at an animal shelter.

What kind of bird can lift the most weight?

A crane

Cranes are not very strong. They are tall slender birds with long necks, long beaks, and long, skinny legs. Cranes usually live in wetlands. They are found all around the world, except in South America. They will eat almost anything, including mice and other small animals. They also eat fish, insects, grains, and plants. The sandhill crane and the whooping crane are the only cranes native to the United States. Both are considered endangered.

The strongest bird is the Andean condor that lives in South America. It has a wingspan of about 10 feet and weighs up to 33 pounds.

If strength is measured relative to body size, then one of the strongest creatures is an insect— the male dung beetle, which can pull 1,140 times its body weight. If this beetle were a person, this would mean lifting close to 180,000 pounds or six double-decker buses full of passengers. Female dung beetles build tunnels into piles of dung, and a male enters a tunnel looking for a mate. If he encounters another male on the way, he has to fight him to get through.

Ants can also carry heavy loads. Some ants actually work in teams to carry large pieces of food back to their nests. This way they can carry more than if they each carried a smaller individual piece.

What animal doesn't know the words to any songs?

A hummingbird

Hummingbirds get their name from the "humming" sound that their fast flapping wings make when they are flying or collecting nectar. Their wings flap at the rate of 60–200 times per second. Hummingbirds do not actually hum, but they make chirping sounds to tell other birds where they are or to warn them to stay away. They are the smallest birds, about 3.5 inch in length, and a hummingbird's eggs are about the size of a jellybean.

Many animals sing to communicate with each other. Most often, it is the males who do so to attract a mate. Scientists define "singing" as sounds made by an animal to attract a mate or to defend its territory. Birds are the best-recognized singers. A nightingale can sing about 300 different songs.

Male humpback whales who live in the same group or "pod" all sing the same song during mating season. Their songs are not just random noises, but have a complex grammar: particular long and short phrases are repeated in patterns. Like a popular song, new versions will spread through the population.

The best love songs come from male bats, say scientists. Like humpback whales, they sing complicated songs with repeated phrases and syllables. Once a male bat convinces a female to join him, he sings a variety of songs to keep her entertained. Only bats can hear these songs because the frequency at which bats sing is too high for the human ear.

What animal is with you at every meal?

A swallow

If you really wanted a swallow with you at every meal, you would have to travel a lot. Swallows migrate: in fall, swallows in the northern hemisphere migrate to warmer climates in the southern hemisphere. When winter begins in the southern hemisphere, they fly back north. The famous swallows of San Juan Capistrano, California spend the winter in Argentina. When spring begins they fly back 6,000 miles to San Juan Capistrano.

Scientists believe that birds can tell when it is time to migrate from the length of the day and the angle of the sun. They also believe that migrating birds can sense the magnetic fields of the north and south poles. It is just like having a built-in compass. Birds also use the position of the sun, the shape of the coastline, and rivers or mountains for navigation. The swallow is a day migrant, but many smaller birds such as rails, warblers, and trushes migrate by night. Birds that migrate through the night use stars to identify north and south. Migration might also be partly learned. More older birds survive migration than younger ones.

To learn where birds go when they migrate, scientists attach a small metal ring or a plastic tag to the leg of a bird. The tag contains information about whom to contact if a bird is found. Today, tiny radio transmitters are sometimes attached to a bird's leg to track its journey and identify its location.

What animal is your aunt afraid of?

An anteater

Ants are a very nutritious food. They are packed with protein. If you are going to eat ants regularly, it helps to have sharp claws to dig into their nests. It also helps to have a long snout that you can stick into the nest, and a long, very sticky tongue to catch the ants. Luckily, these are exactly the features of a giant anteater. Giant anteaters live only in Central and South America. They are about the size of a golden retriever. The anteater's tongue is two feet long, and when eating ants, it can stick its tongue in and out 160 times per minute, eating about 30,000 ants in a day.

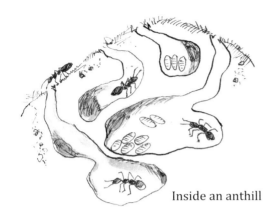
Inside an anthill

An anteater feeds on an anthill for only about a minute. It will then move on to another anthill because the ants will attack to defend their home. The anthill is not totally destroyed and the anteater can come back to feed again another time.

Humans eat ants, too. In areas of the world without lots of large mammals to eat for protein (like cows or pigs), ants are a common food. In Colombia, South America, ants are roasted and salted for eating, like popcorn. This is a favorite movie theater snack.
In Australia the aboriginal people eat honey pot ants. These ants fill themselves up with honey and nectar until they are the size of a grape to bring food back to their fellow ants.

What animal is the worst to play cards with?

A cheetah

Just like someone might try to fool you by cheating in a card game, lots of animals are able to fool other animals by blending into their environments. This is called camouflage. The cheetah's spotted black and tan color helps it to blend in with the tall grasses in Sub-Sahara Africa. Their black spots look like shadows in the grass. This enables the cheetah to sneak up on its prey. A cheetah can run faster than any other land animal—about 70 to 75 miles per hour—but only for a short time. So if the cheetah doesn't catch its prey quickly, the prey will probably escape.

For protection some animals use mimicry: they are able to look like a different animal. The viceroy butterfly protects itself from being eaten by birds by looking a lot like the monarch butterfly, which birds do not like to eat. Other animals are disguised to look like their surroundings: a stick insect, also known as a walking stick, is easily mistaken for a twig.

Chameleons can change their skin color. How is this possible? If the chameleon experiences changes in surroundings or body temperature, this information is transmitted to the cells in its skin. The cells then get bigger or smaller, changing the amount of light that is reflected from the skin underneath. And that changes the color that the chameleon's skin appears to be.

What is a pirate's favorite animal?

A swordfish

The "sword" on a swordfish is actually a long, pointed bill. In some cultures this fish is called a broadbill. To capture a meal, a swordfish swims into a school of fish and slashes its bill about, then eats the ones it has hit. The swordfish can swim as fast as 50 miles per hour, slicing through the water as it swims. There have been rare instances of a swordfish piercing a boat. However, it was not attacking the boat, just swimming so fast that it was unable to stop. Swordfish swim alone instead of in a school, maybe to avoid each other's swords. Since they are so deadly, swordfish have very few predators–just killer whales and humans.

Could the swordfish's bill actually be used as a sword? In Hawaii long ago, when there was no metal available, people carved daggers from the bill. The Chumash, a Native American tribe who lived in southern California, used it as a spear. They also cut the swordfish's vertebrae in half and used them as cups.

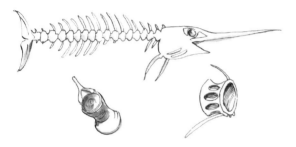

Swordfish's vertebraes and vertebrae "cup" used by the Chumash.

No one knows whether pirates had pets or not. Most sailing ships did have a cat. This helped keep mice and rats away from the ship's food storage. Some pirates may have kept parrots on board for entertainment (since parrots can mimic human words) and to sell once they reached port.

What animal needs a wig?

A bald eagle

Bald eagles are not actually bald. They have white feathers on their heads, and long ago, the word *bald* meant "white-headed." These feathers do not turn white until the eagle is an adult—four or five years old. This may signal to other eagles that the animal is ready to mate. Their white heads also make it easy for other eagles to spot them from far away and to stay out of their territory.

Adult eagles are large, powerful birds with wingspans of about 8 ½ feet. They mate for life and together build a large nest and care for their young.

Bald eagles will eat live or dead animals as well as fish.

Many baby mammals are born furless, but it quickly grows. The babies of marsupials—mammals where the female has a pouch for their babies, such as kangaroos, koala bears and possums—are born very tiny and furless. As soon as they are born they climb into their mother's pouch, where they spend the early months of their lives, safe and warm, drinking her milk and growing fur.

Some animals are bald their entire lives. There are several breeds of hairless cats and dogs, but people who are allergic to cats or dogs still suffer. That's because when people are allergic to cats or dogs, it is usually their skin and saliva, not their fur that causes the problem.

What animal goes best with peanut butter?

A jellyfish

Jellyfish are not made of jelly—at least not the kind you eat with peanut butter. And they are not fish. Most aquariums now call them "jellies." The jellylike substance inside them is called mesoglea, and it is 95 percent water. Jellyfish are the largest type of plankton—a category of sea animals that floats with the sea currents. Although jellyfish can move through the water by moving their muscles, they usually just float.

Many people around the world eat jellyfish. In countries like Japan, China, and Korea, jellyfish are dried, cooked, then cut into thin strips and eaten.

They have a mild taste and are somewhat chewy. Jellyfish have been around for at least 500 million years. The emperor of China ate jellyfish thousands of years ago.

Jellyfish are so plentiful that some scientists think they could become a major food source for humans. They are rich in nutrients like iodine that our bodies need, and they are high in protein and fat free. Jellyfish are found in every ocean. They eat whatever they can catch. Jellyfish can survive where other marine animals cannot, even in very dirty water where oxygen is in short supply.

Not all jellyfish are edible. Some have poisonous tentacles—the strings that trail out from the bell, or the round central part of the jellyfish. If you find a jellyfish on the beach, don't touch it, because even a dead jellyfish can sting.

What animal helps carpenters do their work?

A hammerhead shark

The hammer shape of this shark's head helps it do what sharks do best: hunt for food. Since their eyes are on the far sides of their heads, they can see all around as they look for prey. Their large heads are filled with special sensors that detect the electrical currents of other animals.

A hammerhead shark can find a stingray (its favorite food) hiding under the sand. It can use its wide head to pin a stingray onto the ocean floor. Scientists also think the hammer-shaped head might help it swim better by giving an extra lift to the front of its body.

While hammerhead sharks don't really help carpenters, many animals do help humans in different ways. Seeing-eye dogs help blind people to get around. Service monkeys use their hands to do things for people who are paralyzed. The U.S. Navy trains dolphins to find dangerous mines in the ocean.

Dogs have a sense of smell that is 1,000 to 100,000 times more sensitive than humans. Border guards use dogs to smell if people entering the country have forbidden food or drugs hidden in their luggage. A dog can be trained to smell when a diabetic person's blood sugar is getting low or when someone is about to have an epileptic seizure. Scientists have even trained dogs to detect whether a person has cancer by sniffing their breath.

What animal is the smartest?

Fish, because they spend a lot of time in schools

A school of fish is the name given to a group of fish swimming together, at the same speed and in the same direction. Schooling helps fish to survive, but scientists aren't sure exactly how. It may be that fish can find food faster when they are in schools just like you can find a lost shoe faster when other people are looking for it with you. Schooling probably also confuses predators, who have trouble picking out one fish to target when lots of fish are moving about.

How are fish able to swim together in schools? Schooling is instinctual behavior: fish are born knowing how to do it. Fish school by following their neighbors. They use their eyes, as well as their lateral lines—a row of special cells along each side of their bodies that senses where other fish are. They often have special marks on them that other fish can easily see. Some schools of fish have special names, such as a troubling of goldfish, a run of salmon, a shiver of sharks, and a pod of whales.

How smart are fish? In some areas, like learning and memory, they are as intelligent as non-human primates like apes and monkeys. Non-human primates can use tools, learn to do things, and even communicate with humans using sign language. The smartest animal of all is, of course, a human.

What animal is always ready to take a trip?

An elephant, because it carries its trunk with it

The elephant is the largest land-living animal. There are two types of elephants: the African elephant and the Asiatic elephant. The African elephant is larger. It can grow to about 13 feet tall and has a larger trunk. The Asiatic elephant grows to about 11 feet and has a much smaller trunk.

An elephant can lift and carry things with its trunk. The end of the trunk is sensitive and agile. An elephant can pick up an object as small as a peanut off the ground with the tip of its trunk. The elephant's trunk is like a nose, mouth, and upper lip combined, and it has 150,000 muscles.

Elephants use their trunks to drink, eat, and trumpet—to communicate with other elephants, using loud bellowing sounds. Touching each other with their trunks is another way of communication. To drink, elephants suck water up into their trunks, then pour it onto their mouths. To cool off, they spray the water on their backs. An elephant uses its trunk as a snorkel when it swims underwater. Baby elephants suck their own trunks, just like baby humans suck their fingers

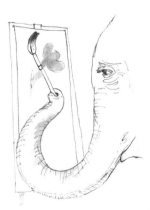

Elephants can paint holding a paintbrush with their trunk. Their paintings have been shown around the world.

What animal is the best to tell a joke to?

A laughing hyena

There are several different kinds of hyenas, but only one that "laughs": the spotted hyena. It makes a high-pitched "hee-hee-hee" sound, like a giggle, when being chased or attacked by lions or by another hyena.

Hyenas live in the grasslands of Africa in clans of 60 to 90 animals, and like other social animals, they use lots of different sounds to communicate with each other. The "laugh" signals frustration, while a low "whoop" sound is used to announce its presence to those far away. Baby hyenas make a "squitter" sound like fingernails on a chalkboard when they want their mothers to let them nurse. Hyenas make lots of different groaning and growling sounds, too. Scientists are just beginning to learn what they all mean.

Are there animals that really do laugh? Yes! Rats laugh (with a chirping sound) when they are tickled. Non-human primates, also called the Great Apes (gorillas, chimpanzees, bonobos, and orangutans), laugh when they are tickled on their bellies or in their armpits, just like humans. Gorillas sometimes tickle each other. In addition, they actually have a sense of humor: they have been known to play tricks on their trainers (like hiding things) and then laughing.

What animal gets a sore throat that goes on for a long time?

A giraffe

Giraffes are the tallest animals that live on land. They can grow as tall as 19 feet! Even though a giraffe's neck is very long, it has only seven supportive bones (called vertebrae) like humans. Their necks are extremely flexible and can turn around 360 degrees. Giraffes' main food is the leaves and flowers of trees—food that other animals cannot reach. Because of their height, giraffes are also able to see predators from far away.

Being tall can be a problem: when a giraffe drinks from a water hole, it has to spread its front legs apart so it can bend down. A giraffe cannot get back up quickly from this position, so it could be attacked by a lion or a leopard. Luckily, giraffes only need to drink water every few days, because they get most of the water they need from the plants they eat.

A giraffe cannot lie down and get up very easily. However, giraffes only need to sleep a few hours each day, so they spend most of their time standing up. Giraffes even give birth to their babies while standing. The newborn calf drops to the ground, but within an hour it can stand up and run.

One newspaper story tells of a sick giraffe, Lucy, who actually had a sore throat. Lucy was cured by squirting medicine through a long tube down her throat.

What animal sleeps with its shoes on?

A horse

Horses wear "shoes" made of metal to protect their hooves from cracking or wearing down. Horseshoes are nailed on to the hoof, but it does not hurt the horse because hooves are like human toenails: they don't have feeling in them. People who put shoes on horses are called farriers, and they are specially trained.

Wild horses do not need shoes. But domesticated horses, who pull loads or carry riders on rough surfaces like gravel and pavements, need horseshoes to protect their hooves. For the same reason, oxen and mules, animals who work pulling or carrying loads, may also be shod (that's the past tense of the verb *to shoe*). Sled dogs wear booties when they race. But it is not because of the cold: the booties protect the dogs' feet from getting scraped on the ice and prevent balls of ice from building up around the footpad.

Thousands of years ago people in Asia made horseshoes out of leather and plants, and Romans in the first century put sandals made of leather and metal on their horses. Europeans in the 6th century were the first to nail metal shoes on horses.

Some people consider horseshoes good luck. Long ago, sailors nailed a horseshoe to the ship's mast because they believed it kept away storms.

What animal is always in a bad mood?

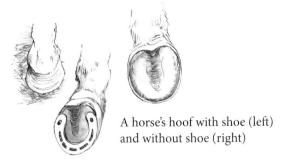

A horse's hoof with shoe (left) and without shoe (right)

A crab

Do animals have moods? Can they be happy or sad? Yes! Scientists believe that nearly all animals experience some basic emotions like fear when a predator is near, and pleasure such as when finding food. Crabs do not feel anger like we do, but they do fight with each other. After a crab molts (sheds its hard outer shell), it must hide while waiting for its new shell to harden. And it may fight another crab for a good hiding place like behind a rock.

Some animals, particularly social animals who need companionship, have more complex emotions. How do we know that? Since animals cannot talk, scientists look at their behavior to identify their moods. Animals may show signs of joy, like jumping around or wagging their tails when they are with their friends and families or when they are playing. They may show deep sadness by staying still, hanging their heads, or refusing to eat. When an elephant dies, its relatives stand around it for days, silently hanging their heads. Some dogs get upset when their owners leave home, so they bark, chew things, jump on the furniture, or scratch the door.

While humans and animals both feel emotions, there is one important difference: humans can think about how they feel, including how they have felt in the past and might feel in the future.

What animal likes to hang around?

A bat

Bats hang upside down when they rest, which is called roosting. They even hibernate upside down. It's comfortable for them, because their weight pulls on tendons in their legs that keep their toes wrapped tightly around whatever they are hanging on to. When a bat is in a hanging position, it can quickly take off flying by just letting go. Hanging upside down means bats can sleep where no predators can reach. When you and I hang upside down, gravity causes blood to rush to our heads. Bats, however, have special veins that keep their blood flowing back up to their feet when they are hanging.

The sloth is another animal that sleeps upside down. Sloths are furry mammals that live in the rainforest in South America. They spend almost all their time in trees, where they sleep hanging upside down—for 18 hours a day! A mother sloth even gives birth upside down in a tree. Some kinds of parrots can sleep hanging upside down, too.

What other animals have strange sleeping habits? Horses sleep standing up. Cows sleep with their eyes open. Dolphins can sleep and swim at the same time, because they shut off only half of their brains while they sleep. Sea otters sleep floating on their backs. They usually wrap themselves in seaweed to keep from floating away. The albatross, an ocean bird, can sleep while it is flying!

What animal gives the best hugs?

An octopus

An octopus has eight tentacles (arms). But unlike the arms of most animals, including humans, each octopus arm has its own "brain": it can problem-solve and coordinate with other arms. Even after an arm is cut off, it will continue to react to stimuli: if it is touched, for example, it curls up. If an arm is damaged or lost, a new one will grow in its place. Scientists call this regeneration.

Some other animals can regrow body parts, too. After their old antlers fall off, deer grow a new pair. Lobsters and crayfish can regrow claws. If a worm is cut in half, the portion with the head may grow a new tail if its vital organs have not been damaged.

The arms of an octopus are covered with two rows of suckers. It uses these to hold tightly onto an object or prey. An octopus can do many things with its arms, too, since it is the smartest invertebrate (animal without a backbone). Octopuses can learn to twist the lids off jars. An octopus named Billy even figured out how to open a childproof medicine bottle. These have tops that you need to press down and turn at the same time.

What animal likes to be in the movies?

A starfish

Starfish, also called sea stars, are often found on beaches. It's their star shape that gives them their name. Most have five arms (rays), but some have more than forty. Some have long rays while others have very short, stubby rays. Starfish are famous for their incredible power to regrow a ray when it is cut off. Even more remarkable, a whole new starfish can grow from a lost ray. The new starfish is exactly like the arm's original owner.

While no starfish has ever been in a movie, animals do star in movies. The most famous was a collie named Pal who played the role of Lassie in

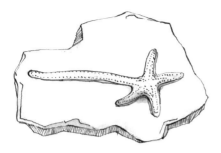

A new starfish growing from a single ray

six popular films in the 1940s and 1950s. The movie *Air Bud* starred a real stray dog who was found by Kevin Di Cicco. Kevin trained Buddy to play basketball, football, soccer, baseball, and hockey. In the movie, several different dogs were used to play Buddy. The calmer ones were in the indoor scenes with humans, and the energetic ones were in the basketball scenes. Using different animals to play one role prevents them from getting too tired.

Dogs are strongly motivated by rewards, so it is easy to teach them tricks by giving them a treat or a pat when they do a good job. Dogs and other domesticated animals like horses bond easily with humans and want to please them.

What animal is good to have around if you run out of batteries?

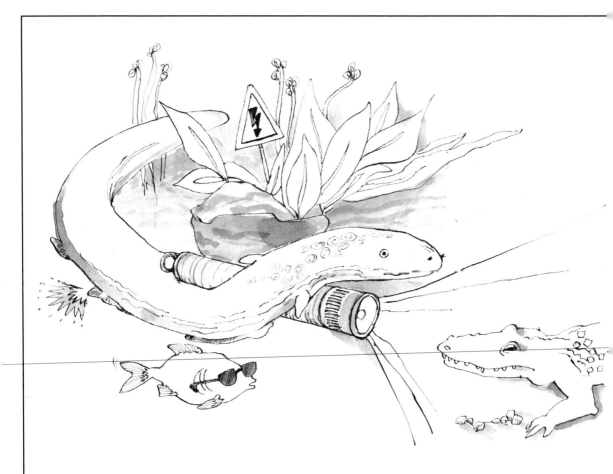

An electric eel

The electric eel is actually a long fish, called a knifefish, that lives in muddy waters in South America. It can grow to be as long as eight feet. The electric eel has no teeth. It doesn't need them, however, because it catches prey and defends itself by shooting out an electric current to shock other animals. Since it has very poor eyesight, it also uses its electricity to find its way around, much like ships and airplanes use radar.

The electricity comes from specialized cells in the fish's body called electrocytes. These cells store power just like a battery does. An electric eel can produce five times the power of an electrical outlet in your house! In fact, some aquariums have used electric eels to power their Christmas tree lights. Metal electrodes are put into the fish tank, which pick up the eel's electric current and transmit it to the lights.

A number of fish produce weak electric currents that they use to navigate in the water. Only a few can shock other fish, and of these, the electric eel has the strongest shock— strong enough to kill a person.

Scientists are studying the electric eel to figure out how to build artificial power cells that copy the way the eel's cells generate electricity. These could be used to power medical implants in humans, like heart defibrillators, without using batteries.